S0-AUS-636

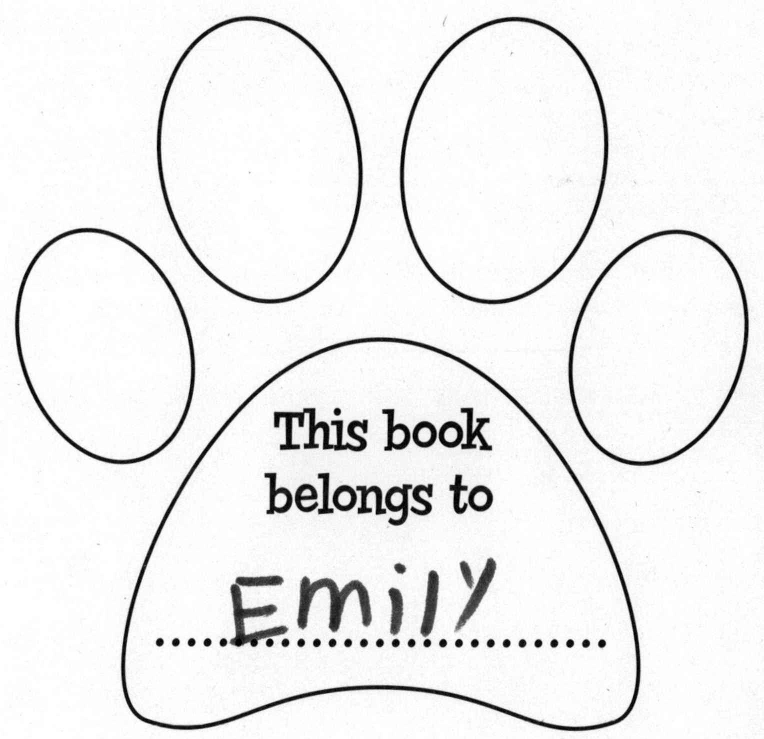
This book
belongs to
Emily

PRINCESS PARTY SLEEPOVER

Cuddle

The Magic Kitten

PRINCESS PARTY SLEEPOVER

by Hayley Daze

This edition published by Willow Tree Books, 2018
Willow Tree Books, Tide Mill Way, Woodbridge, Suffolk, UK, IP12 1AP
First published by Ladybird Books Ltd.

0 2 4 6 8 9 7 5 3 1

Series created by Working Partners Limited,
London, WC1X 9HH

Special thanks to Elizabeth Galloway

ISBN: 978-1-78700-615-7
Printed and bound in Great Britain
by Bell and Bain Ltd, Glasgow

www.willowtreebooks.net

To Daisy and Elizabeth

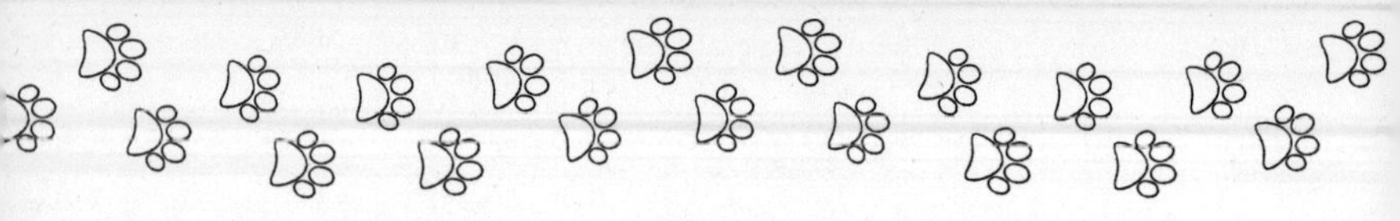

Cuddle the kitten has black-and-white fur,
A cute crooked tail, and a very loud purr.
Her two best friends, Olivia and Grace,
Know Cuddle's world is a special place!

Just give her a cuddle, then everything spins;
A twitch of her whiskers, and magic begins!
So if you see a sunbeam, and hear Cuddle's bell,
You can join in the adventures as well!

Contents

Chapter One
Sunset Surprise

It was a warm summer's evening and Olivia's bedroom window was wide open. Purple wisteria flowers nodded against the sill. Bumblebees buzzed from flower to flower, collecting the last of the day's pollen. The setting sun made the high-rise blocks and houses

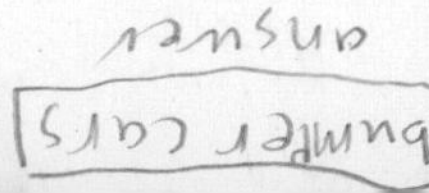

of Catterton glow a rosy pink.

"Our first sleepover!" Olivia squealed, twirling in her pink, ruffled nightdress.

"I've never been to a sleepover before," Grace said, doing up the last button of her favorite star-patterned pajamas.

"Me neither," Olivia said. "What should we do first?" The girls flopped on Olivia's bed, which had a fluffy pink blanket.

"Let's play princesses," Olivia suggested. She leaped to her feet, wobbling on the bed. She wrapped her blanket around her shoulders like a royal robe. "Ta-dah!" she said and pretended to wave at her loyal subjects.

"Hello, Your Highness!" Grace said, bowing to Olivia.

"Now it's your turn," Olivia said, jumping down to sit beside Grace. "You'd make a lovely princess."

Grace shook her head, making her blond ponytail fly about. "No way! Who wants to be a princess and have to wear dresses and go to boring parties? Yuck!"

Olivia stared open-mouthed at her friend. "I would love to be a princess, trying on all those lovely outfits and

tiaras."

Suddenly, the setting sun sent a golden beam of light directly through the open window.

"Maybe Cuddle's coming!" Olivia said, looking down into her backyard.

The girls couldn't wait to see the magical kitten again. Cuddle always arrived in a burst of sunshine and took them on amazing adventures.

Just then, a sound drifted through the window.

Jingle jangle jingle.

"That's her bell!" Grace cried. The wisteria branch beneath Olivia's window was shaking, its flowers bobbing up and down. A tiny white tail flicked out from the quivering leaves, a kink in its black tip.

"Cuddle!" both girls shouted.

The kitten's blue eyes flashed as she scrambled onto the windowsill, the silver bell on her pink collar jangling. She sprang between the girls into Olivia's room, landing in the middle of the bed. "Meow!"

Cuddle bounced onto Olivia's shoulder. Olivia scooped the kitten up, cradling her upside down to show her belly.

"Cuddle's purring," Olivia said, her eyes shining. "That means we're going on another adventure!"

"Where are you going to take us, Cuddle?" Grace asked, nuzzling Cuddle nose-to-nose.

Cuddle's purr grew louder and louder, buzzing like the bees outside. The girls' skin tingled all over, making them giggle. Grace and Olivia squeezed their eyes tightly shut.

"Here we go!" Olivia said.

***

Chapter Two
Treetop Trouble

The girls' eyes fluttered open. Olivia and Grace were still wearing their bedtime clothes and Cuddle had magically given them matching slippers. The evening sky was purple and stars twinkled overhead. A gravel drive stretched before them, edged on

either side by flower beds. The drive ended in a bridge, stretching over what looked like a stream.

"It's a moat!" Grace said, pointing at the sparkling water. "I've heard of those. They were built around old buildings to protect them."

On the other side of the bridge was a grand house, its many windows glittering with a golden light. Music and laughter drifted through an open doorway. On the roof fluttered a red flag with a crown on it, and the number 1853 in swirly lettering below.

"It's a palace," Olivia said, clapping her hands. "And that number on the flag must be the year! Maybe a real

princess lives there."

Cuddle darted up the drive, pausing to look back at the girls. "Meow!" she called.

"OK, Cuddle, we're coming," Grace said, grabbing Olivia's hand.

The girls followed Cuddle across the bridge and toward the palace. Olivia peeked in one of the open windows. Inside was a magnificent ballroom. Glittering chandeliers hung over a dancing crowd, who were moving in time to a four-piece band. Their costumes made a swirling sea of color. Each dancer wore a mask on their face, some decorated with feathers, others shining with jewels.

"It's a masked ball," Olivia whispered as she picked up Cuddle and twirled around and around to the music.

"I'd much rather climb this," Grace said, walking to a nearby tree that was almost as tall as the palace.

Cuddle sprang from Olivia's arms and scampered up the tree. "Meow!" went Cuddle when she reached the lowest branch.

The top of the tree began to sway. Grace peered up through the branches. She thought she saw something. A bird, maybe? Handfuls of leaves rained down on Grace and Cuddle. *A big bird,* Grace thought.

"Pssst, Olivia." Grace waved at her friend.

Olivia danced over to the tree. "What's the matter?" she asked.

"I think someone's in the tree," Grace whispered.

Olivia looked up and spotted Cuddle sitting on the lowest branch. "You mean someone other than Cuddle?"

Grace nodded. The treetop jiggled and wiggled. Olivia clutched Grace's arm. "Maybe it's a thief trying to steal the crown jewels!"

Grace called to Cuddle as quietly as she could. "Please come here, Cuddle."

The kitten blinked her bright blue eyes and then climbed further up the

tree.

"No, Cuddle, come back," Olivia called.

The tree's leaves shuddered and shook. "Maybe the tree is haunted," Grace said.

Suddenly, a figure burst out of the branches high above.

It was heading straight for Cuddle!

Chapter Three
Princess Problems

The strange creature in the tree came to rest on Cuddle's branch. It wasn't a thief or a ghost. It was a girl about the same age as Grace and Olivia. Her hair was in two bunches. Her canvas pants were ripped, her face was smudged with dirt and she wasn't wearing

any shoes.

“Hello!” the girl called.

“How did you get up that tree?” Grace called back.

"I climbed down from my bedroom window," the girl said with a smile. "I do it all the time."

"But why?" Olivia asked.

"I'm hiding," the girl said. "From her!" she whispered, pointing behind Grace and Olivia and ducking out of sight.

A girl in a plain gray dress and a white apron marched straight over to the tree. She was a little older than Grace and Olivia, with brown hair woven into a French braid.

"I know you're up there!" she shouted. "You need to climb down."

"Do you promise I won't have to go to the ball?" the girl in the tree called back.

"You *must* go to the ball, Princess Victoria," the girl in the gray dress said.

"Princess!" Olivia exclaimed. Victoria didn't look like any of the fairy-tale princesses in her books.

"Yes, and if she doesn't go to the ball we are both going to be in big trouble," the girl in gray said. "I'm Beth, by the way."

"I'm Grace. That's Olivia and the kitten's name is Cuddle. Maybe we can help," Grace said.

"That would be great, thank you," said Beth, looking relieved. She lowered her voice so that Victoria couldn't hear. "Princess Victoria never wants to put on her pretty dresses and join in with the royal duties. I don't know why—the masked balls are such fun!"

Grace and Olivia shared a glance. Grace could guess what Olivia was thinking. Olivia felt sure she knew what Grace would say next.

"Cuddle's brought us here to help the princess!" both girls whispered at the same time.

Grace smiled her biggest smile. "I can help get Princess Victoria back to her bedroom," she told Beth. She jumped up, pulling herself onto the lowest branch. "Race you to the top of the tree," Grace shouted to Victoria.

"You're on!" Victoria called back. Within moments, they had both disappeared in the treetop.

"Come on, Cuddle," Olivia called. Cuddle scampered back down the tree and rubbed against the hem of Beth's dress.

"I'll show you to Princess Victoria's

bedroom," the maid said as she started walking toward the palace's main entrance.

"If we work together, I bet we can get the princess to go to the ball," Olivia said.

"I hope so, or the king and queen will be really disappointed," Beth said. "Princess Victoria is finally old enough to stay up for the masked ball so her parents are expecting to see her there."

Beth led Olivia and Cuddle into the palace. A footman bowed as they passed through the big doorway. "Follow me," said Beth, leading the way up a grand staircase with broad marble steps.

They walked down a long corridor, passing marble statues and rows of oil paintings, and stopped in front of a large wooden door. Carved into the surface was the letter 'V'.

Beth looked left and right. "I could get into trouble if anyone sees me near the private quarters. I'm only a maid, after all."

Beth pushed the door open and she,

Olivia, and Cuddle slipped in. Princess Victoria's bedroom was like nothing Olivia had seen before. The carpet was a deep pink, and lilac curtains covered the windows. A dressing table with a pearl-edged mirror was covered with jewelry boxes. On the wall was a glass cabinet filled with glittering tiaras. But Olivia couldn't help noticing the muddy balls and boots hiding beneath the princess's bed, too!

The room had three closets, each with fancy dresses spilling from them. In among all the dresses were a few pairs of canvas pants, perfect for climbing in.

"I win!" Victoria shouted from

the window. The princess and Grace climbed through the window one-by-one and landed with thuds on the floor. As they clambered to their feet, Grace gave Olivia a wink. Victoria looked even dirtier than before.

"Now we can have our own party!" said the princess, grabbing Beth's hands and whirling her around the room. Victoria's face was bright with excitement, but Beth gently pulled her hands away.

"We can't." Beth sighed. "You need to go to the ball and greet your guests."

Princess Victoria looked sad. Olivia could see tears glistening in her eyes.

"It'll be fun!" Olivia said.

Beth took the princess's hand. "Just think how happy you'd make the king and queen."

But the princess sat down on the bed. "Mom and Dad don't understand," she said, staring at the carpet. "They think it's fun, wearing crowns and fancy clothes, but it makes me feel so silly. I wish I could keep them happy, but I just don't want to go!"

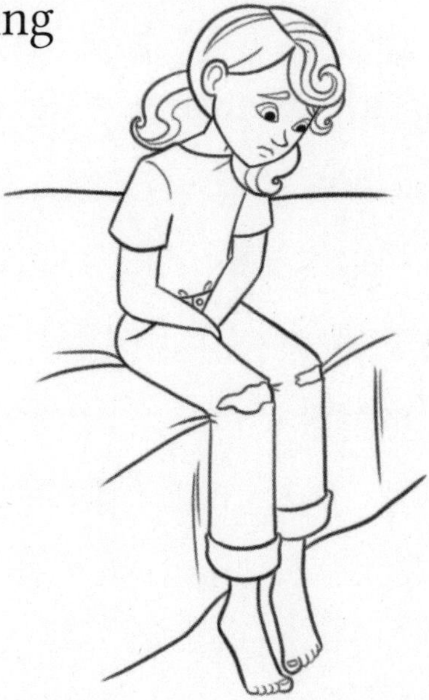

Chapter Four
Feline Fashion Fix

"Meeeeeow!" Cuddle fell out of one of the closets, landing with a *bump* in a tangle of dresses. A silver bracelet nestled between her ears.

"Look, Victoria—Cuddle's a princess, too!" Olivia said.

A small smile appeared on Princess

Victoria's face. "Maybe she could go to the ball instead of me."

Grace hurried over to help Olivia tidy up and whispered in Olivia's ear, "I've got an idea how we can get Victoria to go to the ball."

Grace picked up a silver scarf and knotted it around her forehead. She grabbed an umbrella from one of the closets and swiped it through the air like a sword.

"Ahoy there," she said in a growling voice. "I'm not Grace—I'm a pirate! I sail my ship on the seven seas, and if you don't do what I say, I'll make you walk the plank."

Princess Victoria giggled. "I love to pretend!"

Beth tossed Victoria an umbrella, and Victoria and Grace ran around the room, pretending to sword fight.

Grace lowered her umbrella sword and smiled at Victoria. "You could pretend that you like dressing up and going to balls," she said, in her normal voice.

"It's easy—just imagine you're acting on stage," Olivia added.

"That's a good idea," Beth said. "Go on, Your Highness—just for tonight."

There was a sudden movement as Cuddle paddled around in the pile of dresses. She twitched her whiskers, and a pink dress floated across the carpet. It landed at Olivia's feet.

Princess Victoria gasped. "Cuddle's magic?"

"I think she's deciding what we should wear to the ball," Olivia said.

Cuddle's whiskers moved again. A polka-dot dress moved toward Grace. She held it up and showed the girls the deep pockets on each side. "It's like my cargo pants back home."

Next, Cuddle pushed against Beth's ankles, nudging her toward a shimmering blue gown covered in sparkly sequins. Beth's eyes shone as she picked it up.

Then the little kitten sat beside a red dress embroidered with tiny flowers. The sleeves were edged with ribbons and it had an underskirt of red lace. Cuddle stared at Princess Victoria.

"Why don't you try it on?" Grace asked.

Princess Victoria picked up the dress. "It's all...frilly. Do I really have to wear it?"

Cuddle threw back her head and yowled. "Meeeeeooowwwooowww!"

"I think that's a yes," Olivia said, laughing.

But Victoria shook her head and dropped the dress onto the floor. "Sorry, Cuddle. Dressing up just isn't any fun!"

Olivia's heart sank. How could they persuade the princess to go to the ball?

Chapter Five
Dressing-up Fun

Cuddle crept toward the princess's bare feet. She shook her head so her whiskers brushed over them.

"Hee hee!" giggled Victoria.

Grace turned to Olivia and Beth. "I think Cuddle's got a plan," she whispered excitedly.

The kitten swished her curly tail against Victoria's ankles.

"That tickles!" the princess squealed. Cuddle flicked her tail again and Victoria spun away from Cuddle, shaking with laughter. The princess was happy again.

"It's like you're dancing!" Grace cried, watching Princess Victoria skip and leap around the room to escape Cuddle's tickles.

Victoria stopped in her tracks. "Dancing would be fun." The princess glanced at the dress that Grace had grabbed from the floor.

Grace yanked down the zipper and held it out, the opening of the dress gaping wide. "Just give it a try," she said. Cuddle meowed gently as if she was saying the same thing.

After a few moments, Princess Victoria gave a nod. "All right, then!"

Olivia and Beth helped the princess climb out of her canvas pants while she hopped from foot to foot, laughing. Grace waited for Victoria to step into the dress, then—zip!—she fastened the back up.

"That was great," the princess said. She knelt down and stroked Cuddle's silky head. "I didn't know dressing up could be so much fun."

"Does this mean you'll go to the ball?" Grace asked.

Princess Victoria frowned. But then a smile tugged at the corners of her mouth. "OK," she said. "I'll do it. I'll go to the ball. But only if you three come with me—and you, Cuddle." Princess Victoria stroked Cuddle from the top of her head to the black tip of her tail.

"Of course we will!" Olivia cried. Princess Victoria grinned. "And after the ball, we can have a sleepover."

"Hooray!" Grace and Olivia cheered.

Olivia picked up the pink dress and shrugged it over her head. Grace and Victoria did up the tiny buttons at the back, while Beth arranged the dress so it hung properly. Even Cuddle tugged the frilly edges with her teeth, pulling them straight.

Then Grace stepped into the polka-dot dress, and the other girls did up the hook-and-eye fastenings. Victoria picked up the blue sequinned dress.

"It's your turn, Beth," she said.

"I'm not sure—" Beth began. But Olivia held the dress against her, covering her maid's uniform. "You're going to look so pretty," she said.

"All right, then." Beth took off her uniform, folding it neatly and placing it on the bed. She gazed shyly at the carpet as Grace and Victoria buttoned the dress up.

The four girls stood together in front of the pearl-edged mirror. Their dresses shimmered.

"We look like princesses," Olivia said.

But a sob broke from Beth and a tear trickled down her cheek. "I'm not a princess. I can't go to the ball. If anyone recognizes me, I could get into big trouble."

Grace and Olivia shared a doubtful glance.

Victoria folded her arms. "We can't go without Beth."

Chapter Six
Four Princesses

"Meow!" went Cuddle as she leaped into an open jewelry box. She twitched her whiskers and a cloud of gold glitter descended over the girls. As it drifted to the floor they gazed at each other in amazement. They were all wearing masks, magically given to them by

Cuddle! Each mask was a different color, to match the girls' dresses. The eye slits were almond-shaped, and whiskers made from feathers were glued beside the ridge of the nose. On the top of each was a pair of pointed ears.

"Cat masks!" Olivia cried.

Grace took Beth's hand. "They're the perfect disguise," she said. "No one at the ball will know we're not all princesses."

"Please say you'll come," Princess Victoria begged.

Beth smiled. "I will! I'll be a princess for one night."

The four girls grabbed each other's

hands, skipping around in a circle.

Knock knock knock.

The girls froze. Cuddle's ears flicked toward the door.

"Come in!" Princess Victoria called.

The door opened and an elderly man in a black suit and white gloves stepped inside.

"Are you ready, Your Highness?" he asked. His watery eyes widened as he saw the other girls, and he bowed. "I beg your pardon. I didn't realize that other young ladies were present."

Princess Victoria winked at Beth. "See?" she whispered. "Even Graves the butler doesn't recognize you." She spoke louder. "Graves, please may I introduce

Princess Olivia, Princess Grace...and Princess Elizabeth."

The butler gave a deep bow. "It's an honor to meet you," he said, straightening up. The girls could hardly stop smiling.

Cuddle jumped onto the floor and rubbed against the butler's polished shoes.

"Are you ready to go to the ball, little one?" he asked.

"We're all ready, Graves," Princess Victoria replied. "Including Cuddle." Graves coughed. "Forgive me, Your

Highnesses, but aren't you forgetting something?"

"Of course," Victoria cried. "Tiaras!" She opened the cabinet and passed a tiara to Olivia, Grace, and Beth, before choosing one for herself. Each tiara was covered with sparkling diamonds. Graves helped the girls fit them behind the pointed ears of their cat masks.

"I feel like a real princess now," Olivia whispered to Grace.

The girls followed Graves down the corridor, carefully holding up the hems of their dresses so they wouldn't trip. They went down the grand staircase, beneath the sparkling chandeliers, and then down another corridor that led to the ballroom doors. They stood before the huge varnished doors and smoothed down their silk skirts. Grace peeked at Princess Victoria and saw her face blushing with pleasure, the tiara sparkling on her head. Graves opened the door and they stepped inside, among the whirling dancers.

"What do we do now?" Princess

Victoria asked.

"Enjoy ourselves!" Olivia cried. She pointed to a group of boys and girls gathered on the other side of the ballroom. "Let's go and say hello."

Grace tucked Cuddle into one of the deep pockets of her dress and the girls weaved through the crowd.

As they were passing the band, a man in a bear mask shot his elbow out, knocking into Beth. The ribbons tying her mask in place fell loose, revealing part of her face.

"Oh, I'm so sorry, Your Highness!" the man cried.

"It's all right," Beth said. But her fingers trembled as she tried to refasten the ribbons.

"Here," Olivia said, swiftly knotting them. She hoped no one had recognized Beth.

"Oh, no," Beth muttered and ducked behind Olivia and Grace. The girls glanced up to see the king and queen heading their way. Olivia and Grace fanned out their dresses and stood on their tippy-toes trying to hide Beth, but it was too late.

The king and queen walked right up to them. The girls curtsied. Beth tried to keep her head down.

"Victoria," the king said when he reached his daughter, "aren't you going to introduce us to your friends?"

Grace swallowed. Were they going to be in trouble for bringing Beth to the ball?

Chapter Seven
The Star Dance

"This is..." Princess Victoria started but her voice was shaking. "Princess Olivia and Princess Grace who have come to visit from a far away land. And..." She looped her arm through Beth's. "This is..."

"Yes, of course, it's your friend

Beth," the queen said.

"I am so sorry," Beth said in a shaky whisper. She ducked in a quick curtsy.

"Sorry?" the queen repeated, glancing at her husband. "Why are you sorry? Victoria loves being with you and we're so glad to see you enjoying the ball."

The queen hitched up her velvet skirt so that she could kneel beside the girls. Her eyes were sparkling and a golden crown rested on her head, among her blond curls.

She wore an emerald bracelet on her wrist and around her waist was a green silk sash. "I'm so glad you've brought Victoria here," she whispered. She looked from Grace, to Olivia, and back to Beth. "The three of you must be very special girls indeed."

The king helped his wife back to her feet, nodding in agreement. He was wearing a crown too—it looked very heavy on his head. His waistcoat was embroidered with gold thread and his jacket was made of gold satin.

"Enjoy yourselves!" he cried, flinging out an arm to take in the ball. "That's what tonight is all about." Then the two of them disappeared into the crowd, nodding and smiling to people.

Cuddle wriggled out of Grace's pocket, darting through the legs of the dancers. Princess Victoria chased after her, dancing between people. She scooped the little kitten up in her arms.

"Oh, Cuddle!" she gasped. "You're leading me on a dance again."

A crowd of boys and girls in animal masks gathered around Victoria and Cuddle.

"I've always wanted to meet a real princess," a little girl in a butterfly mask said.

Princess Victoria's eyes flicked between Olivia and Grace, as if she didn't know how to reply. Grace cupped her hand and whispered in the princess's ear.

Victoria nodded at Grace, and then spoke to the girl. "And I've always

wanted to meet a butterfly. What an amazing mask!" The girl gave a delighted squeal. Princess Victoria chatted to all the other children, turning to Grace and Olivia when she wasn't sure what to say.

Olivia bobbed her head in time to the music, making her curls bounce. "Let's dance!" she cried. The four girls held hands and twirled to the music, their dresses billowing out so they looked like spinning tops. Cuddle scampered among their feet. She paused for a moment and wiggled her whiskers, and thousands of tiny glittering silver sparkles cascaded over the girls.

"It's like we're dancing in a cloud of stars!" Princess Victoria cried. The girls danced and danced until their cheeks shone, their satin slippers moving quicker and quicker across the varnished wooden floor.

"This way!" Olivia called, leading the others in a gallop across the ballroom, winding in and out of the swirling crowd.

The song came to an end and the girls collapsed onto a set of golden chairs, giggling and gasping for air.

Somewhere in the room, a trumpeter sounded a fanfare and a loud voice boomed out. "Their Royal Majesties would like to give a speech!"

The crowd of guests parted as the king and queen stepped through the room. Two servants placed thrones beside the band and the king and queen swept toward them, waving to the crowd.

"Come on," Princess Victoria said, leaping up from her seat. She pulled the other girls to their feet and began to race through the crowd. The girls ran over to the raised platform, where the king and queen sat.

The king cleared his throat and spoke loudly enough to be heard by everyone at the ball. "It is my pleasure to present to you all my daughter, Princess Victoria, on the occasion of her first royal masked ball." The king reached for his daughter's hand and she stood up on the stage next to her parents. Everyone cheered as Princess Victoria waved to the crowd.

"Victoria, we're so proud of you for coming to the ball," the king whispered to his daughter. "We know you don't usually like this sort of thing."

"My friends showed me that it's nice to try something new," the princess said, smiling at the girls. Her eyes suddenly widened. "But I'll still be allowed to climb trees, won't I?"

"Of course," the queen said. "We would never stop you from being who you are."

The king stroked his beard, looking at the grandfather clock that stood by the wall. "It's almost midnight," he said. "Time for bed."

Princess Victoria grinned. "Bedtime's the best time of all."

Chapter Eight
Sweet Dreams

The four girls sat cross-legged on Victoria's bed. Victoria, Grace, and Olivia were wearing their bedtime clothes.

"The ball wasn't so bad," Victoria said, "but sleepovers with friends are more fun!"

Beth was still wearing her blue sequinned dress. "I think I'm going to keep it on a bit longer," she said.

Beside Victoria's bed was a golden platter of fruit—juicy slices of pineapple, a pile of ruby cherries, delicious oranges, and tiny plates of raisins. On a small card was a note in beautiful writing. It read:

To some very special girls. Enjoy your feast (and don't stay up too late!). Love, the King and Queen

Cuddle curled up on a comfy pillow at the foot of the bed as the girls dug into their feast.

After they had eaten, Olivia shook out her black curls and Beth wove them

into a French braid. Grace and Victoria pretended to be sword fighters again, but finally fell on the bed laughing.

"I've had so much fu-u-u-un," Princess Victoria said, her words turning into a yawn. "Thank you so much for helping me today." She stretched her arms and lay down against the pillows.

Beth curled up beside her. "I'll never forget meeting you two and Cuddle," she murmured, her eyes drifting closed.

The room was quiet except for the soft sound of their breathing. Grace and Olivia carefully climbed off the bed.

"I've had a wonderful time," Olivia whispered. She rubbed her eyes. "But

I’m feeling sleepy too.”

Cuddle jumped off the pillow, and flicked her tail. As she wound through their legs, the girls felt the familiar tickling sensation.

“It’s time to go home,” Grace said.

***

When the girls opened their eyes, they were back in Olivia’s bedroom. Cuddle perched on the chest of drawers.

Olivia smiled at Grace. “Didn’t I say you’d make a lovely princess?”

Grace laughed. “It was fun to do

something different," she said. "Maybe tomorrow you could try wearing my cargo pants."

Olivia nodded. "I'll even accessorize them with boots and a backpack," she said. "If Victoria can do it, so can I!"

Both girls gave loud yawns. Cuddle jumped down, touching her nose to Grace's in a goodnight kiss. She did the same to Olivia and hopped onto the windowsill.

"Goodnight, Cuddle!" both girls cried. "See you soon!"

The little kitten disappeared in a puff of sparkles, which shimmered over the girls like stars.

“Goodnight,” Olivia murmured drowsily.

“Goodnight,” yawned Grace in reply, “Sweet dreams!”

Can't wait to find out what Cuddle will do next? Then read on! Here is the first chapter from Cuddle's fourth adventure, School of Spells...

SCHOOL OF SPELLS

Olivia squeezed her eyes shut.

"Abracadabra, fiddle-dee-dee, show me my wand, as fast as can be!"

She opened them again and looked at the dressing-up box on the lawn of her backyard. A pirate hat, face paints, and a pink feather boa were spilling out

out of it, but Olivia sighed.

"I can't see my wand anywhere," she said to Grace.

The two girls were in fancy dress. Olivia's fairy outfit was a purple leotard and tutu and pink net wings covered in silver sparkle. Her mom had made the outfit for Olivia on her sewing machine. Slung over her shoulder was the little bag she took everywhere.

Grace was dressed up as an elf, in green shorts and a T-shirt, and plastic pointy ears hooked over her real ones.

"Don't worry," Grace said, "my mom says I'm good at finding things. When we lived on a farm, I used to look for where the chickens had laid their eggs.

I'll help you find your wand."

It was a gray day in Catterton, with clouds squatting low over the houses and high rise blocks. Olivia and Grace had decided to brighten up the backyard, turning it into a fairy grotto. Olivia had strung daisy chains from the branches of the trees, while Grace had lined up her mom's garden gnome collection on top of the fence.

The girls knelt beside the potted plants on the paving, searching among the leaves and flowers.

"If only I was a proper fairy," Olivia said. "Then I could use magic to find it."

Grace jumped up, her eyes shining. "We do know someone with real magic."

"Cuddle!" Olivia cried. The girls grinned at each other. Cuddle was a magical kitten who took them on amazing adventures.

Just then, a beam of sunlight reached through the clouds. It shimmered in the air like a golden rainbow, shining right onto the dressing-up box.

Jingle jangle jingle.

"That's Cuddle's bell!" Grace cried. "She's here!"

The girls ran toward the dressing-up box and looked inside. Its contents wobbled and quivered, and a black-and-white tail with a kink in its tip poked through. Then came a pair of black paws, and finally a furry white face.

"Cuddle!" Olivia exclaimed. "And look what she's found."

The kitten had a plastic purple wand in her mouth. Olivia tucked it inside her bag.

"Clever Cuddle," Grace said, and tickled the kitten on the belly, just where her purr was rumbling.

With a meow Cuddle sprang into Grace's arms, the silver bell on her pink collar jangling. Both girls shut their eyes as the kitten's purr made their skin tingle all over.

"I feel like I'm covered in fizzy sherbet," Olivia murmured. "I wonder where Cuddle will take us this time..."

***

Grace rubbed her eyes. They were standing on a large stretch of grass. White stripes marked out a sports field and on the edge of the grass was a school building with iron gates and lots of little windows winking in the sunlight. Grace could hear shouts of

laughter and chatter coming from a play area to the side of the building.

"Why would Cuddle bring us to a school?" she said to Olivia. "We go to one of these all the time."

The kitten jumped down from Olivia's arms, and scampered across the grass toward the cries of other children. But as the girls stepped inside the play area, they gasped with amazement.

"These aren't children!" Grace cried, gazing around her. The friends held

hands and turned in a slow circle, their eyes grew wide as they took everything in.

"Weeeee!" shouted a pixie, kicking with his curly-toed shoes as he whizzed down a slide. The pixie jumped off the slide, and Olivia could see that he only came up to her waist.

A group of elves, dressed in green, were playing soccer with a small ball against a team of gnomes. "Goal!" yelled one of the elves. "Good shot!"

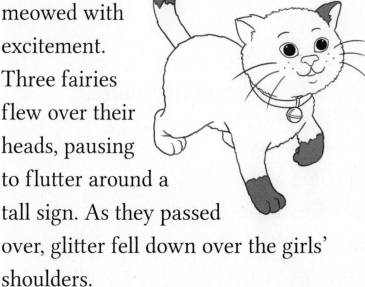

"I don't believe it," Olivia whispered. "Look!" She pointed into the air above and Cuddle meowed with excitement. Three fairies flew over their heads, pausing to flutter around a tall sign. As they passed over, glitter fell down over the girls' shoulders.

Olivia shook the glitter from her hair and laughed. Gazing back up at the sign, she saw golden letters painted on it.

"Miss Rosamund's School for

Magical Creatures," she read out loud. Olivia turned to Grace, her eyes bright. "We're at a school for magic!"

To be continued...

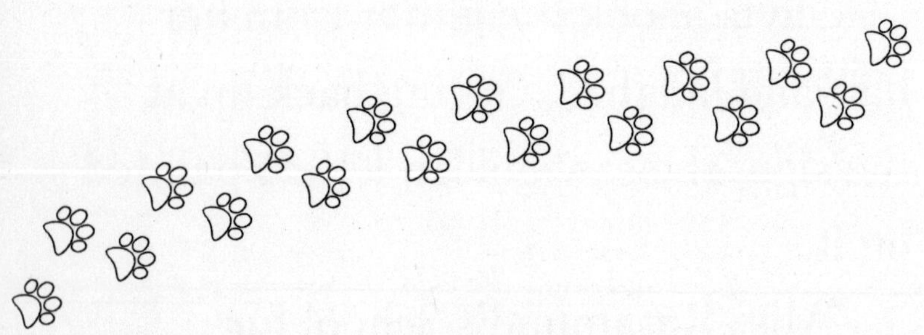

Cuddle
The Magic Kitten